SECRET AGENTS
JACK & MAX STALWART

THE BATTLE FOR
THE EMERALD BUDDHA:
THAILAND

BOOKS BY ELIZABETH SINGER HUNT

THE SECRET AGENT
JACK STALWART SERIES

BOOKS BY ELIZABETH SINGER HUNT

THE SECRET AGENTS
JACK AND MAX STALWART SERIES

Book 1–The Battle for the Emerald Buddha **(Thailand)**

Book 2–The Adventure in the Amazon **(Brazil)**

Also:
The Secret Agent Training Manual:
How to Make and Break Top Secret Messages

And:
Swamp Mysteries: The Treasure of Jean Lafitte

For more information visit
www.elizabethsingerhunt.com

THE BATTLE FOR
THE EMERALD BUDDHA:
THAILAND

Elizabeth Singer Hunt
Illustrated by Brian Williamson

WEINSTEIN
BOOKS

Cataloging-in-Publication data for this book is available from the Library of Congress.

ISBN: 978-1-60286-359-0 (print)
ISBN: 978-1-60286-360-6 (e-book)

Published by Weinstein Books
A member of Hachette Book Group
www.weinsteinbooks.com

Weinstein Books are available at special discounts for bulk purchases in the U.S. by corporations, institutions and other organizations. For more information, please contact the Special Markets Department at Perseus Books, 2300 Chestnut Street, Suite 200, Philadelphia, PA 19103, call (800) 8104145, ext. 5000, or e-mail special.markets@perseusbooks.com.

First edition

LSC-C

10 9 8 7 6 5 4 3 2 1

For Eve, who had the "master" idea

GLOBAL PROTECTION FORCE: INTERNAL MEMO

After successfully protecting King Tut's priceless diadem in Egypt, Secret Agents Courage and Wisdom have decided to retire from the force.

We wish them well in their next adventures and hope that they will consider joining the GPF again soon.

Gerald Barter

Gerald Barter
Director, Global Protection Force

THINGS YOU'LL FIND IN EVERY BOOK

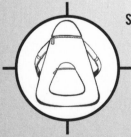

Global Protection Force (GPF): The GPF is a worldwide force of junior secret agents whose aim is to protect the world's people, places, and possessions. It was started in 1947 by a man named Ronald Barter, who wanted to stop criminals from harming things that mattered in the world. When Ronald died, under mysterious circumstances, his son Gerald took over. The GPF's main offices are located somewhere in the Arctic Circle.

Watch Phone: The GPF's Watch Phone is worn by GPF agents around their wrists. It can make and receive phone calls, send and receive messages, play videos, unlock the Secret Agent Book Bag, and track an agent's whereabouts. The Watch Phone also carries the GPF's Melting Ink Pen. Just push the button to the left of the screen to eject this lifesaving gadget.

Secret Agent Book Bag: The GPF's Secret Agent Book Bag is licensed only to GPF agents. Inside are hi-tech gadgets necessary to foil bad guys and escape certain death. To unlock and lock, all an agent has to do is place his or her thumb on the zipper. The automatic thumbprint reader will identify him or her as the owner.

GPF Tablet: The GPF Tablet is a tablet computer used by GPF agents at home. On it, agents can access the GPF secure website, send encrypted e-mails, use the agent directory, and download mission-critical data.

Whizzy: Whizzy is Jack's magical miniature globe. Almost every night at 7:30 p.m., the GPF uses him to send Jack the location of his next mission. Jack's parents don't know that Whizzy is anything but an ordinary globe. Jack's brother, Max, has a similar buddy on his bedside table named "Zoom."

The Magic Map: The Magic Map is a world map that hangs on every GPF agent's wall. Recently, it was upgraded from wood to a hi-tech, unbreakable glass. Once an agent places the country shape in the right spot, the map lights up and transports him or her to their mission. The agent returns precisely one minute after he or she left.

THE WORLD

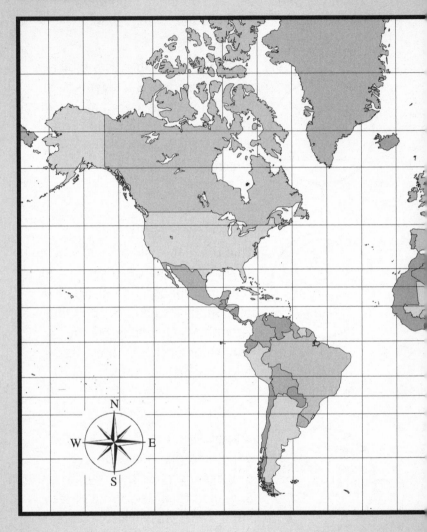

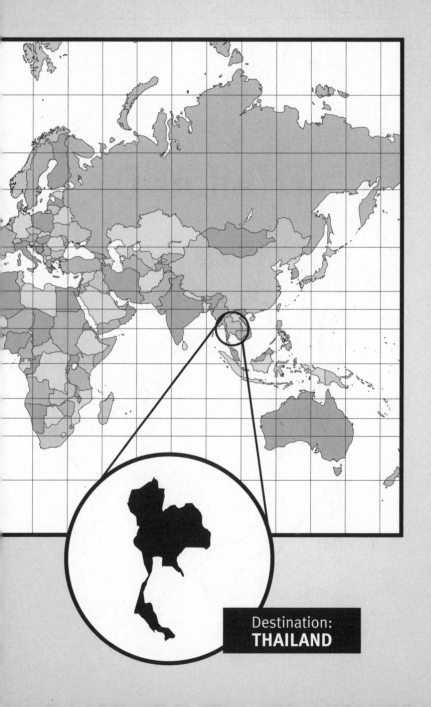

Destination:
THAILAND

THAILAND

BANGKOK

ANDAMAN
SEA

DESTINATION: THAILAND

Thailand is located in Southeast Asia. Its capital city is Bangkok, which Thai people call Krungtep.

Thailand used to be called Siam. Siamese cats originated in Thailand.

Elephants are sacred symbols in Thai society. They're respected for their strength and intelligence.

Thailand is home to the world's smallest mammal (the bumblebee bat) and the largest fish (the whale shark).

The official language of Thailand is Thai. Its currency is the baht.

EMERALD BUDDHA: FACTS AND FIGURES

🌸 The majority of Thai people practice Buddhism.

🌸 There are more than 40,000 Buddhist temples in Thailand.

🌸 The most famous is the Temple of the Emerald Buddha at the Grand Palace in Bangkok. Inside is a statue called the Emerald Buddha.

🌸 The Emerald Buddha is two feet tall and made of a green, semiprecious stone.

🌸 It wears a different gold outfit depending upon the season. The above illustration shows the Buddha in its "cool season" attire.

🌸 Before entering the temple, you must take off your shoes.

🌸 The Emerald Buddha is sacred to the people of Thailand. Without it, the safety, security, and spiritual well-being of the country would be in jeopardy.

SECRET AGENT PHRASEBOOK FOR THAILAND

FUN FACT: Thai language has forty-four consonants, thirty-two vowels, and five tones.

CRYPTOGRAPHY 101

If you're going to be a secret agent, you'll need to disguise your top secret messages. One way to do this is to use a "Caesar cipher" (pronounced *Cee-sar Si-fer*).

It's a trick named after the ancient Roman general, Julius Caesar, who used this method to keep his military strategies safe. Instead of using letters from the normal alphabet, he used letters from a made-up cipher alphabet. These letters were three places to the right of the normal.

Here's how to create a Caesar cipher:

Draw a grid with two rows and twenty-seven columns. Fill in the top row with the letters of the normal alphabet. Fill the bottom row with letters that are three places to the right of the normal. Instead of "A," your cipher alphabet will start with "D."

Normal	A	B	C	D	E	F	G	H	I	J	K	L	M	
Cipher	D	E	F	G	H	I	J	K	L	M	N	O	P	

Your grid should look like the example at the bottom of the page.

Let's say you wanted to send the message "HELP."

Find the letter "H" in the normal row, and write down the letter underneath. It's "K." Do the same for "E," "L," and "P." The Caesar cipher for "HELP" is "KHOS."

To solve, all your fellow agent would have to do is the reverse. He or she would find the letter "K" in the cipher row and write down the letter above it. It's "H." They would then do the same for "H," "O," and "S." Eventually, they'd come up with your original message saying "HELP."

To discover more tricks for hiding your top secret messages make sure to read *The Secret Agent Training Manual: How to Make and Break Top Secret Messages*.

N	O	P	Q	R	S	T	U	V	W	X	Y	Z
Q	R	S	T	U	V	W	X	Y	Z	A	B	C

THE STALWART FAMILY

Jack Stalwart: Nine-year-old Jack Stalwart used to work as a secret agent for the Global Protection Force, or GPF. Jack originally joined the GPF to find and rescue his brother, Max, who'd disappeared on one of his missions. Jack tracked Max to Egypt, where he saved him *and* King Tut's diadem, or crown. After that, Jack and Max retired from the force. The brothers live with their parents in England.

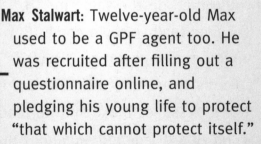

Max Stalwart: Twelve-year-old Max used to be a GPF agent too. He was recruited after filling out a questionnaire online, and pledging his young life to protect "that which cannot protect itself." Max's specialty within the GPF is cryptography, which is the ability to write and crack coded messages. Recently, Max narrowly escaped death in Egypt, while protecting King Tut's diadem. After Egypt, he and his brother, Jack, decided to take a break from the GPF.

John Stalwart: John Stalwart is the patriarch of the family. He's an aerospace engineer, who recently headed up the Mars Mission Program. For many months, the GPF had fooled John and his wife, Corinne, into thinking that their oldest son, Max, was at a boarding school in Switzerland. Really, Max was on a top secret mission in Egypt. When that mission ended, Max's "boarding school" closed, and he returned home for good. John is an American and his wife, Corinne, is British, which makes Jack and Max a bit of both.

Corinne Stalwart: Corinne Stalwart is the family matriarch. She's kind, loving, and fair. She's also totally unaware (as is her husband) that her two sons used to be agents for the Global Protection Force. In her spare time, Corinne volunteers at the boys' school, and studies Asian art.

Chapter 1
The Mastermind

In an office somewhere in Europe, a well-dressed sixty-year-old man sat at his desk. His cold, calculating eyes peered at the priceless objects across from him.

A glittering Fabergé egg sat on a wooden coffee table. Picasso's famous painting, *The Acrobat*, leaned against a bookcase. Rare coins from a shipwreck lay perched on a shelf.

The man was in the presence of
greatness. But none of these items
belonged to him. He'd stolen them from
their owners and planned to sell them
for lots of money.

He opened a desk drawer and pulled
out a cell phone. This was no ordinary
phone, but a prepaid or burner device
that prevented the police from tracing his
calls. The man quickly tapped out a coded

text and pushed the "send" button.

Now all he had to do was sit back and relax. If all went according to plan, within twenty-four hours, another one of the world's most precious treasures would be his.

Chapter 2
The Gang

In an abandoned building in Bangkok, Thailand, three teenage boys were talking to one another. The oldest boy, Grill, was the gang's leader. Grill loved to wear black. His long, stringy hair was black. His clothes were black. Even his belts and shoes were black. The only thing that wasn't was the menacing silver brace or "grill" that he wore over his top four teeth.

The second-oldest teen, Shark, had an obsession with Great Whites, which is why he styled his hair in a fin. The youngest member of the group was a skinny genius named Tech, who knew all about the latest high-tech gadgets. Tech was so thin that his pants were constantly slipping off his hips.

Together, the teens had become a successful gang of thieves. Their specialty was stealing priceless works of art.

Recently, the gang had stolen Van Gogh's *Starry Night* painting from a museum in New York City. They'd managed to swap the original with a fake when nobody was looking.

The reason they were so successful was because of their use of hi-tech gadgetry and parkour. With parkour, the teens could jump over obstacles and scale walls. Not only was the gang unidentifiable, they were uncatchable.

The only person who'd discovered their identity was the man who'd hired them to steal the *Emerald Buddha*. In exchange for stealing the statue, he promised them three business-class tickets to Thailand from America and

$300,000 in cash. A few weeks ago, he'd taught the gang how to communicate using coded messages. Although they'd traded messages with the man, none of the boys had ever met him.

PING!

A coded text arrived on Grill's smartwatch. He quickly deciphered it and turned to the others.

"He wants us to take the statue at 4 p.m.," said Grill.

Tech made sure the folding table, film plate, and laser were in his bag. Shark had the grappling hooks.

"Remember," said Grill, strapping his empty black backpack over his shoulders. "If we get caught, nobody talks."

The gang gave one another a fist bump. Then, they slinked out into the busy streets.

Chapter 3
The Past

Nine-year-old Jack Stalwart was sitting in an airplane 30,000 feet in the sky. He and his family were on their way to Thailand, a country in Southeast Asia. Jack and his twelve-year-old brother, Max, were by the window. Their parents, John and Corinne, were sitting across the aisle.

Max leaned over Jack, and pointed to a patch of land below.

"See that," he said. Sunlight streamed in from the window, causing Max's blond hair to look gold. "That's India," explained Max. "I went there to stop someone from putting graffiti on the Taj Mahal."

Jack knew all about the Taj Mahal. This mausoleum was known as the "jewel of India." The closest that Jack had ever gotten to India was on his mission to Nepal. There, he tried to protect a yeti skull from a Russian curio collector.

Jack and his brother, Max, used to be secret agents for the Global Protection Force, or GPF. As GPF agents, they were assigned to protect the world's most precious treasures. During his four months with the agency, Jack had stopped countless villains from destroying things that mattered in the world.

In Australia, he prevented a bunch of pirates from plundering the shipwreck of the HMS *Pandora*. In France, he captured the crooks responsible for stealing the *Mona Lisa*. When a master illusionist tried to take the Queen's Crown Jewels in England, he foiled that attempt too. In Russia, Jack saved his father from a madman wanting to send an unsafe rocket to Mars. (Thanks to the GPF's Memory Eraser, however, Jack's dad didn't remember a thing.)

The reason Jack joined the GPF in the first place was to find his then-missing brother, Max. Max was a GPF agent who'd disappeared on one of his missions. Jack traced Max to Egypt, where he'd been trying to protect King Tut's diadem, or crown.

Unfortunately, a crooked archaeologist wanted to use the crown's power for

sinister reasons. Thankfully, Jack, Max, and another agent (Kate Newington) stopped him. They bravely fought an army of giant scorpions to rescue King Tut's diadem and the Egyptian people.

After that mission, Kate returned to her life and the GPF, while Jack and Max decided to take a break. They wrote to Gerald Barter, the director of the GPF, and told him they wanted to retire for a while.

The boys returned their Book Bags, Watch Phones, Magic Maps, and miniature globes. For Jack, the hardest part about quitting was giving up his little friend, Whizzy. Whizzy was the animated gadget that gave Jack the location of his missions.

But there were benefits to no longer being an agent too. Jack didn't have to worry about bad guys anymore. In fact, his only mission on this trip to Thailand was to relax. With that in mind, Jack reclined his seat and closed his eyes. There was a fun-filled vacation ahead of him and he had to get some last-minute sleep.

Chapter 4
The Grand Palace

After checking into their hotel, the
Stalwarts hopped on a ferry boat and
headed north on the Chao Phraya River.
The Chao Phraya was Thailand's biggest
and busiest river. All kinds of boats plied
the river as it snaked through Bangkok.
There were river taxis, ferry boats, long-
tail boats and big teak barges. Local Thai
people often used the Chao Phraya as a
way to escape the smoggy, traffic-filled
streets.

After twenty minutes, the Stalwarts arrived at the Ta Chang pier. They stepped off the boat and made their way through a noisy food market. Soon, they found themselves standing at a busy intersection and facing their first destination—the Grand Palace.

The Grand Palace used to be the home and workplace of the Thai royal family. Now, it was a tourist destination in Bangkok visited by millions of people each year.

"They weren't kidding when they called it 'grand,'" said Max.

The Grand Palace covered an area of more than

two million square feet. The complex was guarded by a low white wall. In addition to containing beautiful walkways, gardens, and pieces of art, the Grand Palace included many well-known buildings. The most famous was the Temple of the Emerald Buddha because it housed a sacred green statue called the *Emerald Buddha*.

Jack and Max knew all about the idol.

The statue had been on the GPF's list of the "World's Most Precious Treasures" since the list began.

Jack and his family stood staring in awe at the complex.

Because many of the buildings were painted in gold and covered in glass mosaics, the Grand Palace was literally twinkling in the sunlight.

"What are we waiting for?" said John. "Let's go inside!"

The Stalwarts crossed the street, bought their tickets, and entered the Grand Palace.

Chapter 5
The Temple of the
Emerald Buddha

Corinne pulled out the map of the grounds. "Where to?" she asked.

Max leaned over her shoulder and pointed to a building on the map marked with a "1." "Let's go and see the *Emerald Buddha*," he said.

In the near distance, Jack could see the temple. Like the rest of the buildings at the Grand Palace, it was glistening.

Thousands of mirrored mosaics covered the walls and a band of gold-painted creatures called *garudas* wrapped themselves around the middle. Jack wasn't sure about Max, but he couldn't wait to see the legendary idol inside. As they approached, they noticed a giant green-faced statue with bulging eyes. This was a *yakshi*, or guardian of the Temple of the Emerald Buddha.

Corinne took out her cell phone. "Gather up!" she said, motioning for the boys to stand next to the statue.

Jack and Max playfully put their arms around each other and mugged for the camera. Corinne snapped a photo.

Before entering the building, John, Corinne, and Max put their shoes on a shelf outside. Jack, however, was struggling to take his off. There was a knot in one of his laces.

"You guys, go ahead," he said, waving his family on.

As Jack bent down to untie the knot, someone burst from the temple and knocked him to the ground.

"Watch it," growled Jack.

When Jack looked up, he was surprised to see a teenage boy rushing passed. The boy had black hair, black clothes, and was wearing a black backpack over

his shoulders. He was
followed by two other
teens. One had hair
styled in the shape of
a shark's fin, while
the other was skinny
with baggy pants.
None of the teens
were looking at Jack

or anyone else for that matter. Their eyes
were focused on the ground.

"Strange," muttered Jack.

Jack debated whether to follow the
teens. After all, he wanted to tell them
off for being so rude. But Jack's family
was waiting for him. So, instead, he
brushed himself off, untied his lace, and
stepped through the open doorway and
into the temple.

Chapter 6
The Small Wonder

As soon as Jack did, he gasped. The *Emerald Buddha* was sitting at the back, perched on top of a tiered pedestal. The statue was wearing delicate gold clothing with a pointed gold headpiece on its head. Although the idol was small—only two feet tall—it commanded respect.

In addition to the Stalwarts, there were eight other visitors inside. Everyone was kneeling on the floor, praying with their chins down and their eyes closed. Jack squeezed in next to Max, and began to pray too.

But almost as soon as he did, a piercing scream ripped through the temple.

Jack's eyes sprang open. A middle-aged Thai woman was standing at the front. She was jabbing her finger at the pedestal, and shouting something in Thai.

Jack wasn't fluent in the language, but the GPF had taught him enough to recognize the words "Buddha" and "empty."

When Jack looked to the pedestal, he immediately understood why the woman was upset. There was nothing on top. The *Emerald Buddha*, one of the world's most precious treasures, was gone.

Chapter 7
The Dirty Trick

One by one, the visitors stood up. They scanned the room for signs of the statue. A Japanese tourist rubbed his eyes, as if he'd just woken from a dream.

"I don't understand," said Corinne.

"Where did it go?" asked John.

A German woman standing next to them offered a suggestion. "Maybe," she said, "someone took it down to clean it."

It was a nice idea, but Jack didn't buy

it. There wasn't enough time for someone to climb the pedestal, remove the statue, and leave without anyone noticing. It had disappeared within seconds.

"Perhaps it fell," suggested the Japanese man.

Jack thought that was unlikely too. After all, they would have heard it crash to the floor. But an Australian man walked to the back of the pedestal anyway.

"The headpiece is here," he cried out from behind the perch. "But there's no sign of the Buddha."

Jack could see the tip of the headpiece lying by itself on the floor. This wasn't good news. Jack turned to his mother. "Can Max and I have a look around?" he asked.

"Sure," said Corinne. "But don't go too far."

Jack and Max walked from the pedestal

and along the west wall. Almost immediately, they came upon a wooden folding table.

"That's odd," said Max, thinking the table looked out of place.

There was framed piece of glass on top and a small laser light underneath. As soon as Jack and Max saw these items, they knew exactly what had happened to the *Emerald Buddha*.

"It was stolen," said Max.

"And the crooks," added Jack, "used holographic imaging to do it."

Chapter 8
The Nasty Teens

A holographic image was a floating three-dimensional image. Jack and Max had learned about holographic images during their GPF Tech Camp. In fact, they'd learned how to make one using a film plate, laser, and special chemicals.

Once an image was recorded on a plate, you could project it later on by shining a laser on it. For years, magicians had used tricks like holography to make images appear on stage when they weren't really there.

"Whoever took it," whispered Max, "projected an identical image of the Buddha over the real one."

"Then when the real one was taken," said Jack, "nobody noticed."

"Unfortunately for the thieves," reasoned Max, "the hologram disappeared when the laser rolled off the table."

Something was baffling Jack. "Why didn't anyone see the crooks?" he asked.

"Everyone's eyes were closed," offered Max. "It would have been easy for them to take it while people were praying."

The question now wasn't "how" the statue disappeared, but "who" had taken it.

Jack and Max examined their suspects.
There were twelve people in the room,
including the Stalwarts. None of them
seemed to have the Buddha with them.

"The thief must have stolen it before

we arrived," suggested Max. "Maybe they carried it out in a bag."

Just then, Jack remembered something. A teenage boy with black hair had barreled into him as he was entering the temple. The boy was wearing a large black backpack. He and his friends had their eyes to the ground. At the time, Jack thought they were being moody teens. But now, he wondered if their behavior was on purpose. Maybe they were trying to hide their faces.

Jack excitedly grabbed Max's arm. "I think I know who did it," he said. Jack told Max about the teens and their odd behavior.

"They definitely sound suspicious," said Max.

In the near distance, Jack could hear high-pitched whistles and stomping feet coming their way.

"It's the police," said Max. "What do you want to do?"

The boys thought about waiting for the authorities. But Jack and Max didn't speak fluent Thai, and there was a chance the cops wouldn't believe them. After all, they were just a couple of ordinary kids. They no longer worked for the GPF.

If the teens did steal the *Emerald Buddha*, they were only a few minutes ahead. Jack and Max thought that if they left now, there was a chance they could catch them.

"Follow my lead," said Max as he led Jack back to their parents. Max turned to his mother.

"Jack and I need to go to the toilet," said Max.

"Now?" said Corinne, confused. "It's not the best time."

Jack tried his best to look "uncomfortable."

"Oh, all right," said Corinne. "But make it quick."

Jack and Max bolted from the temple, just before twenty Thai policemen

arrived. Twelve of the men covered the exits. The others made their way toward the visitors. The cops pointed to the

ground and shouted something in Thai.
John, Corinne, and the others sat
down. Corinne desperately looked to the

exits. "I hope they're okay," she said to John.

"They'll be fine," said John, putting his arm around his wife. "I'm sure Jack and Max will be back in a flash."

Chapter 9
The One That Got Away

But Jack and Max weren't coming back.
At least not without the *Emerald
Buddha*. As soon as they got outside,
they grabbed their shoes and started to
run.

"Which way?" asked Max.

"Give me a second," said Jack as he
dashed for the giant *yakshi*.

The last time Jack had seen the crooks,
they were heading north. He clambered

to the top of the statue's base and looked in that direction.

Jack didn't have real binoculars, so he used his hands to make fake ones. He put the tips of his fingers together and looked through the holes.

Near the white wall surrounding the palace, he spied the teens. They were pulling climbing devices called "grappling hooks" out of their bags. Holding on to the rope end, the teens threw the barbed end over the wall. As soon as the hook dug itself into the top, the boys began to climb.

"They're taking the Buddha over!" hollered Jack.

Jack jumped down from his

perch. He and his brother sprinted for the teens.

"Stop!" shouted Max as they ran.

But the crooks ignored them. They kept on climbing.

The kid with the baggy pants reached the top of the wall first. He pulled his rope up and over. Then, he disappeared to the other side. The kid with the fin did the same. The boy with the black hair, however, was still climbing.

Jack double-timed it. He headed for the wall and leaped for the rope.

BLAM!

The jolt of Jack landing on it caused the teen to nearly lose his grip. The teen regained his

footing and angrily glared down at Jack.

"Get off my rope!" snarled the teen.

"Never!" said Jack as he scrambled up after him.

The boy raced to the top. As soon as he got there, he looked down to the other side. With Jack on the rope, the teen couldn't use it to lower himself to the ground.

"Jump!" shouted one of his accomplices.

The black-haired crook swung his feet up and over

the wall. He held onto the barb as he let his feet dangle twenty feet off the ground. Jack reached up and grabbed his wrist.

"Gotcha!" said Jack, as he wrapped his fingers tightly around the kid's watch.

But instead of looking worried, the boy grinned up at Jack. It was then that Jack saw the evil-looking grill in his mouth.

"I don't think so," he spat in an American accent.

Then the boy swiftly jerked his wrist.

SNAP!

And fell from Jack's grasp.

Chapter 10
The Fake-Out

Jack looked down, expecting to find the boy in a crumpled heap on the ground. But instead, the teen was now sprinting without injury from the palace with his friends.

Just then, Jack felt something hard in his hand. He looked down to find the teen's watch staring back at him.

"That's what snapped," said Jack.

But Jack didn't have time to look at

the watch. He stuffed it into his pants
pocket for later.

By now, Max had joined Jack at the top
of the wall. The brothers watched as the
teens slid across car hoods, jumped over
road cones, and leaped over trash bins.

"They know parkour," said Max.

Jack and Max expected the
teens to slip into a
getaway car. But
instead, they
headed for the
market across
the street.
When Max
remembered
what was on the
other side, his face
dropped.

"The Chao Phraya River," said Max.
"They're going to escape by boat."

Chapter 11
The Revealing Clue

The brothers knew that if the thieves got onto the river, there was almost no chance of tracking them down. The Chao Phraya River was 200 miles long.

Jack and Max pulled out their cell phones. No signal. Their English phones didn't work in Thailand. If they did, they could have called the GPF for help. Instead, Jack and Max were on their own.

The brothers swiftly rappelled down the wall. They crossed the street and sprinted for the market. As soon as they got inside, they looked for the crooks. But they were nowhere to be found.

Up ahead was a sign for the Ta Chang pier. They headed for it and raced down the ramp. There, sitting in a long-tail boat at the dock were the thieves.

Two of the teens were strapping down their bags, while the skinny teen was sitting at the back. As soon as he saw Jack and Max, he warned the others.

"We've got company!" he hollered.

Max ran for the boat and dove off the pier. Unfortunately, the kid at the back thrust the propeller in the water. The boat shot from the dock just before Max could land in it. Instead, Max fell face-first into the water.

SPLASH!

His blond-haired head broke above the surface. The teens cackled as they sped away. Max swam back to the dock. Jack gave his brother a hand and helped him out onto the platform. The brothers watched as the thieves headed up the Chao Praya and disappeared around the bend.

With the crooks gone and no way to follow them, Jack and Max had no choice but to give up. At least they could give the police a description of the boys.

"What do you say we get a snack from the market?" said Jack. Jack didn't have any Thai baht, so he hoped the seller would accept British pounds. He reached into his pocket for the money. But when  he did, he found something else. The teen's watch.

"I'd totally forgotten about this," said Jack, as he pulled it out. He showed it to his brother.

As Jack flipped it over, the boys noticed something strange on the screen.

"It's a cipher," said Max.

A cipher was a kind of coded message that used a random mix of letters, numbers and symbols.

The boys weren't sure whether it had anything to do with the theft of the

Emerald Buddha. But they had to find out. Luckily for them, Max was an expert in cryptography, or the art of making and breaking coded messages.

WLJHUZRUOG
5SR

Max carefully studied the text. It looked like it could be a Caesar cipher.
A Caesar cipher was a type of message

that used letters three places to the right of the normal alphabet. It was named after the ancient Roman military general, Julius Caesar, who used the trick in battle.

Max borrowed a piece of paper and a pencil from a soda seller nearby, and drew a grid with two rows and twenty-seven columns. He filled the top row with the "normal" alphabet and the bottom row with a "cipher" alphabet three places to the right. Instead of starting with "A," the cipher alphabet started with a "D," and circled back around to end in a "C."

One by one, Max found the letter from the cipher in the cipher row and wrote down the letter above it. For "W," he wrote a "T." For "L," he scribbled an "I." And so on. He left the number "5" alone. Eventually, he got:

WLJHUZRUOG

5SR

Normal	A	B	C	D	E	F	G	H	I	J	K	L	M
Cipher	D	E	F	G	H	I	J	K	L	M	N	O	P
Normal	N	O	P	Q	R	S	T	U	V	W	X	Y	Z
Cipher	Q	R	S	T	U	V	W	X	Y	Z	A	B	C

TIGER WORLD

5PM

He couldn't believe it. Not only did the message "Tiger World 5 p.m." make sense, "Tiger World" was the name of a famous tourist attraction in Bangkok. Hundreds of people visited every day to see dangerous Bengal tigers performing tricks.

If Max was correct, then a meeting was about to take place there. Max scrolled through the watch's text history to see who had sent the text. But the message history had been wiped clean, and the sender's information was blocked.

Max glanced at his own watch. It was 4:40 p.m. "We need to hurry," he said. "The meeting's in twenty minutes."

In the distance, the boys spied a long-tail boat speeding up the river. Jack and Max furiously waved their hands. The driver spotted them and within seconds, he'd pulled his boat up to the dock.

"*Sua lok*," said Jack, telling him "Tiger World."

The driver told them it would cost them thirty Thai baht.

The brothers didn't have any Thai money. But Jack had his British pounds. He pulled out a £5 note. As soon as the man saw it, a smile spread across his face. It was worth seven times what the man was asking for.

The driver took the money, and helped the boys into his boat. Within seconds, the boat blasted from the pier. The boys were on their way to Tiger World.

Chapter 12
The Stealth Move

The man was going at least sixty miles per hour. The buildings on both sides of the river were whirring past, and the skin on Jack and Max's cheeks was being pulled back to their ears. The brothers laughed at how silly they looked.

"I guess £5 buys you speedy service!" hollered Max over the noisy engine. At least Max's wet clothes were starting to dry in the wind.

After crossing under a bridge, the driver hung a right down a narrow canal. He cut his speed in half, and Jack and Max found themselves in a peaceful community.

There were stilted wooden houses on both sides with children playing on the banks. Two five-year-old boys did a cannonball from their dock, trying to splash Jack and Max as they passed. The brothers waved to them. The boys giggled and waved back.

After a few minutes, Jack spied a sign suspended over the canal.

As they approached, Jack noticed a dock in the water and a gravel car park between the pier and the backside of Tiger World. Oddly, there was only one vehicle—a truck—in the car park.

"That's weird," said Jack. "I thought it would be busier."

Max motioned for the driver to cut the engine. The boat quietly drifted toward the pier. As soon as they butted up against it, the boys crawled out. Jack and Max hid behind a couple of garbage cans. The driver and his boat disappeared up the canal.

The brothers kept low and made their way for the truck. They crouched down beside it, looking for anyone or anything suspicious ahead.

"Clear," said Jack, telling Max it was safe.

The boys went another twenty yards

and put their backs to the building. Jack and Max peered around the corner. Satisfied that no one was there, they scurried down an alleyway and headed for the entrance. There, they were greeted by a surprising sign.

ปิดซ่อม

CLOSED FOR REPAIRS

Chapter 13
The Meeting
Between Thieves

The boys weren't sure whether Tiger
World was really closed for repairs, or
whether the teens had arranged for
nobody to be there. Either way, they
needed to get inside—and fast. It was
five o'clock.

Above the double sliding glass doors
at the entrance was a small pitched roof.
On either side of that were cream-colored

walls covered in flowering vines.

The brothers used the stalks of the vines like rungs of a ladder and scrambled to the top of one of the walls. From there, they had a bird's-eye view of Tiger World.

A circular tiger performance ring was in the center of the attraction. Surrounding that was a high fence. Around that was tiered seating for the audience. Four paths led to and from the performance area. One led to the exit. Another led to the café. The last two went deeper into the park.

Scattered around Tiger World was an assortment of trees, bushes, snack carts, benches, and water fountains. There were also seven large tiger pens with one Bengal tiger in each. As far as Jack and Max could tell, the tigers were safely locked inside.

"Any sign of the teens?" asked Jack, peering through the leaves at the top of the wall.

"Not at the front," said Max. "Let's check the back."

Jack and Max lowered themselves onto a nearby picnic table and joined a path leading deeper into the park. Every twenty yards or so, they tucked themselves behind a tree, so they wouldn't be seen. Along the way, they kept their ears pricked and their eyes open for the teens.

In the near distance, they heard voices. They scurried toward a tool shed and hid themselves behind it. Peering around the corner, the boys spied the teens talking to a middle-aged man. Jack pulled out his camera and started to film the conversation. Jack and Max didn't recognize the man, but they could tell he was up to no good.

The man had evil-looking tattoos on both of his arms and a leather vest studded with skulls. His face was worn with age and he wore a permanently furrowed brow. Except for the stubble on his face, there was no hair on his head.

The man's intimidating looks, however, didn't seem to bother Grill.

"I'm Grill," he said, pointing to his

chest. He thumbed toward the kid with the fin-shaped hair. "That's Shark. And that's Tech." For the last name, Grill gestured to the skinny kid with the falling-down pants.

Jack thought they were pretty good nicknames. They fit with what the boys looked like. But the man was less generous.

"Those are stupid names," he grunted with a heavy British accent.

Grill's eyes narrowed. "Then what's *your* name?" he asked.

The man rolled his eyes. He paused for a second. "Larry," he answered.

Jack didn't think it was his real name. Neither did Grill.

"Okay, *Larry*," said Grill. "Do you have the money?"

The man unzipped his backpack and showed the boys what was inside. There were at least thirty stacks of $100 bills, which meant there was about $300,000 in the bag. Jack's and Max's eyes bulged. Grill and the teens barely blinked.

"Where's the idol?" asked Larry.

The teen unzipped *his* bag to show the man what he had. A flash of green and gold caught the sun. It was the *Emerald Buddha.*

"What are you going to do with the statue?" asked Grill.

"I'm just here to collect," said Larry.

"So you're not the guy who hired us?" asked Grill, looking disappointed.

Larry shook his head. "I was paid to pick it up," he grunted.

Jack couldn't believe it. Neither the teens nor Larry was behind the theft of the Buddha. That meant there was someone else in charge. He (or she) was probably the one who'd sent the text.

Jack and Max now had the evidence they needed. It was time to arrest the crooks and rescue the *Emerald Buddha*.

Chapter 14
The Deadly Twist

Jack stepped out from behind the shed. He held his hand out like a crossing guard.

"Stop," command Jack.

Larry was confused. He wasn't expecting another kid.

"Who are you?" snarled Larry.

"I'm your worst nightmare," said Jack. It was a bit dramatic, but he'd always wanted to use that line.

Max came out from behind the shed
and joined Jack. "You heard my brother,"
said Max.

"What's with the ankle
biters?" asked Larry, tilting
his head toward Jack and
Max.

"Ignore them," said Grill
dismissively. "They think
they're cops."

Larry laughed. Grill's nasty
sense of humor clearly
appealed to him.

"If you give these guys
the money," said Jack to
Larry, "you're going to jail."

"Is that so," growled Larry.

"Pretty much," said Jack.

Jack pulled out his phone. He showed
Larry the video he'd captured—the one
with him negotiating for the Buddha in

exchange for the cash in his bag.

As soon as Larry saw it, his face turned red with rage. Beads of sweat formed on top of his shiny dome-shaped head.

"You little—" said Larry, trying to grab the phone.

Jack swiped it away before Larry could get it. He stuffed his phone back in his pocket.

"It's no use," said Max. "We've already sent a copy to the police."

Jack gave a sideways look to his brother. This was a lie. Their cell phones didn't work. But Larry didn't need to know that.

"If anything happens to us," said Max, "they'll use facial recognition software to track you down."

Max figured Larry's mug shot was in at least a few police databases around the world.

"In fact," said Jack. "The police are already on the way."

The color drained from Larry's face.

"Don't listen to 'em," said Grill. "They're trying to mess with you. Give us the cash and you can have the statue."

"I, uh—" said Larry.

Jack and Max's plan to sow seeds of doubt was working. Larry was hesitating. Grill sensed it too. He whispered something to Shark.

"Change of plans," announced Grill. "We're going to find another buyer."

Larry looked surprised.

"But we're going to take the cash anyway," said Shark.

Before Larry could react, Shark ripped the bag of cash off of Larry's back and sprinted for the exit. So did Grill and Tech.

"You two-timing little thieves!" shouted Larry as he went after the money.

"I'll get Grill!" hollered Max as he ran after the kid with the Buddha.

"I'll take Shark!" said Jack.

But Shark wasn't easy to get. Just when Jack reached out for the teen, Shark leaped onto the back of a bench with one foot and catapulted himself ten feet from it.

"Give me back my money, you fool!" shouted Larry as he tried to catch up to Shark too.

Unfortunately for Larry, a lifetime of cigarette smoking had taken its toll. He was wheezing so hard he had to stop. Larry hugged a nearby water fountain.

Jack ran around the bench and tried to cut Shark off by taking a different path. But Shark went right and thrust his hands on top of a snack cart. He lifted himself up and over the cart, putting another obstacle in Jack's way.

Max wasn't having any luck either. Grill was proving impossible to catch. Max decided to try a different approach. He scooped some gravel off the ground and threw it ahead of Grill's path. When Grill came down, he slipped on the rocks. His feet came out from underneath, and he landed on his backside.

Max snatched the bag from Grill. As he was about to strap the backpack to his shoulders, Tech appeared from behind.

There was a hi-tech gadget in his hand, and he was pointing it at Max.

When a small red light appeared on Max's back, Jack panicked. He tried to warn his brother.

"Max!" hollered Jack. "Watch out!"

But it was too late. Max's body seized up, and he fell to the ground, motionless.

Chapter 15
The Payback

"No!" shouted Jack as he abandoned Shark and ran for his brother.

"No amount of money is worth this," muttered Larry, after seeing what had happened to Max. Larry slinked toward the exit and left.

Grill snatched the backpack from Max and planted it firmly back on his shoulders. Then, he crouched down to make sure Max could see him. Grill's cold green eyes were level with Max's panicked blue ones.

"You shouldn't have come after us," said Grill. "And now you're going to pay."

The teens ran off and disappeared from view. Jack arrived at Max, just as the teens left. He gently scooped Max's head off the ground and held it in his hands.

"You're going to be all right," said Jack, stroking his brother's blond hair. He hated to see Max looking defenseless. "It was just a Paralaser."

A Paralaser was a hi-tech device that could instantly paralyze someone's muscles. Jack knew all about it because the GPF had added one to their Gadget Directory before they'd retired. The good news for Max was that its effects didn't last long.

"You'll be back to normal in five minutes," said Jack.

Just then, Jack heard a strange series of sounds from around the bend.

CLANG!

CLANG!

CLANG!

"I'll be back," said Jack as he left Max to explore the source of the sound.

As soon as Jack rounded the bend, he froze. Standing in his path were three Bengal tigers.

And they were licking their chops.

ROOOAAAAARRRR!

Chapter 16
The Near Miss

Payback from Grill, Jack thought, for messing with the teens' plans.

Jack thought of Max lying helplessly on the ground behind him. He had to do whatever was necessary to keep the tigers away from Max.

Jack looked around for something, anything that could help. Ten yards to his right was a snack cart on wheels. Because of the pictures of salty snacks on the side, he figured there might be something in there that he could use.

One of the male tigers was getting antsy. It was snarling at Jack.

"Easy, buddy," said Jack, putting his hand out.

Keeping his body facing the tigers, Jack slowly walked backward to the cart. He bumped up against it, and felt for the top with his hands.

"Please be unlocked," he said to himself as he gripped the edge.

He tugged on the top. It opened. Using his peripheral vision, he looked inside. There were bags of peanuts, potato chips, and beef jerky. He grabbed several bags of jerky and ripped them open with his teeth. Jack threw them at the tigers.

The tigers pounced on the snacks. Within seconds, they'd wolfed them down.

"Drat," thought Jack. He needed something that would last longer.

Just then, Jack spied a glass-topped freezer near the backside of the performance ring. He'd seen these types of freezers before in sweet shops in England. Usually, there were Popsicles and ice-cream bars inside. Jack wasn't sure whether the tigers liked desserts, but it was worth a shot.

Jack snatched another handful of jerky, opened the bags, and tossed them as far as he could. The tigers went after the food.

With the animals distracted, Jack sprinted for the

freezer. He looked through the glass top and noticed that instead of ice-cream pops, there were frozen hunks of meat.

"Meat pops!" said Jack. He grabbed three of them.

Unfortunately, the tigers saw them too. They started to charge at Jack!

Jack hurled the bones as far away as possible, and dived behind a nearby bench for protection.

BLAM!

BLAM!

BLAM!

The tigers hit the dirt, then double backed in the direction of the pops. With the tigers now running in the opposite direction, Jack made a beeline for his brother. Luckily, Max was sitting up when Jack returned. He was groggy, but feeling better. Jack scooped his brother off the grass.

"We have to get out of here!" hollered Jack.

Max's muscles sprang into action. The Stalwarts sprinted for the exit.

Unfortunately, one of the male tigers noticed them. It began to chase Jack and Max. It was only seconds behind them.

"Hurry!" shouted Max.

The tiger was closing in.

"The exit!" hollered Max, as they aimed for the glass door ahead.

Max grabbed the handle and flung it open. The boys dove inside to the floor. They looked over their shoulders and watched the tiger in terror.

As the door began to close, Jack and Max could see the animal's crazed eyes zeroing in on them. Its paws were reaching out with every stride. Luckily, the glass door closed, just before the tiger could reach them. Instead, the beast skidded to a stop and plastered its face on the glass.

ROOOAAAAARRRR!

Chapter 17
The GPF's Buddy

The tiger wasn't happy.

He snarled at the boys. Then, he strutted off.

As soon as the brothers caught their breath, they turned around. Jack and Max found themselves in a gift shop surrounded by hundreds of tiger-related knickknacks. There were tiger stuffed animals, tiger key chains, tiger magnets, tiger necklaces, and tiger banks.

On the opposite wall, Max spotted something. It was an old-fashioned pay phone. The boys had seen these kinds of phones on street corners in England.

"We can call the GPF," said Max. "Maybe they can locate the teens."

Unfortunately, they needed money to make the phone work. Neither Jack nor Max had any Thai coins. Then, Jack had an idea.

"We can call collect," said Jack as he ran to the phone and lifted the receiver.

Jack dialed a "o" for the operator. When the Thai woman answered, he told her that he wanted to place a

"collect call." That meant that Jack didn't have to pay for it. The person on the other end did.

Luckily, the woman spoke English. She understood Jack. He gave her the number of the GPF's secret emergency hotline. It rang only once before someone on the other end picked up. The operator spoke first.

"I have a collect call from Thailand," she said. "Will you accept?"

The voice on the other end responded immediately.

"Yes, I will," it said.

Jack recognized the voice. It was Buddy Rogers. Buddy was an older man from the United States, who'd been at the agency for nearly twenty years. The operator hung up. Jack was now speaking directly with the GPF.

"Hi, Buddy," said Jack. "This is Secret

Agent Courage."

Even though Jack no longer worked for the agency, the GPF's voice recognition software identified him as a trusted, former agent.

"What can I do for you, son?" asked Buddy.

"My brother and I have been chasing the crooks that stole the *Emerald Buddha* in Thailand," said Jack.

"I see," said Buddy, sounding surprised and impressed.

"Unfortunately," said Jack, "we've lost them. Could you help us out?"

"Sure thing," said Buddy. "Where were they last seen?"

"Tiger World," said Jack. "There were three thieves. Two of them were wearing black backpacks."

"Let me see if I can find them," said Buddy. Jack could hear Buddy typing on a keyboard. "Bear with me for a few minutes, while I send out a drone."

The GPF had recently dispatched thousands of drones, or remote-controlled flying devices, to key locations around the world. The GPF's drone could take photos and videos, see through walls, and recognize faces.

Any images needed could be sent directly to an agent's Watch Phone. But since neither Jack nor Max had theirs anymore, Buddy was going to have to tell them what he saw.

"I've got 'em," said Buddy. "They're running for the floating market two miles due east from you."

"Thanks," said Jack. "We're on it."

"In the meantime," offered Buddy, "I'll contact the Thai police and recall our other agent. There's no use sending someone if the two of you are on the case."

"Thanks," said Jack. "You should also tell animal control that there are three tigers on the loose at Tiger World."

"Will do," said Buddy, without missing a beat. "Nice to have you back, Secret Agent Courage."

"Nice to be back," said Jack before he hung up.

Max looked at his brother. His eyebrows rose. "Nice to be back?" he echoed. "I thought we were *retired*."

Jack shrugged his shoulders and smiled.

Chapter 18
The Floating Market

A three-wheeled motorbike taxi called a
tuk-tuk was sitting in front of Tiger
World. Its male driver was taking a break
and eating *satay*, or grilled chicken on a
stick. Jack and Max left Tiger World and
hurried over to him.

"*Talad na*," said Jack, telling him they
needed to go to the "floating market."

Jack pulled the remaining £5 out of his
pocket and showed it to the man. As

soon as the driver saw it, he welcomed the boys inside. Jack and Max jumped in and within seconds, they were off.

They'd been traveling for five minutes when the brothers spotted the teens. The crooks were on foot, sprinting along the road to their left.

Jack pointed to the boys and motioned for the driver to pull over. The driver swerved to the left and skidded to a stop in front of the thieves. Jack and Max locked eyes with the Gang. Grill's upper lip curled. Then, the teens made a break for it.

They dashed around the taxi. Jack and Max jumped out and started chasing after them. Ahead was a sign for the floating market. The crooks hooked a left and disappeared underneath it. Jack and Max followed.

The market was total chaos. It was difficult for Jack and Max to locate the teens. There was a busy canal of boats in front of them and hundreds of tourists all over the place.

"Over there!" said Max, pointing to a long dock to their left.

The gang was running along it. Nearby, an elderly Thai lady was about to step into a boat. There were several fruit baskets inside.

Grill shoved her aside, knocking her to the ground. The thieves jumped into the boat and took off. Tech was at the back steering it down the canal.

Jack and Max ran over to the woman. They helped her up.

"*Kawp khun ka*," she said.

But Jack and Max didn't have time to chat. They had to get a boat of their own.

"If we lose them in the canal," said Max, "we'll never find them."

There was an arched pedestrian bridge to their right. It was directly over the canal that the teens were on. Jack and Max made a beeline for it.

They arrived just as the teens were about to travel underneath. Jack and Max didn't need to count to three. They jumped on one.

Chapter 19
The Pet Python

It was a perfect landing. Max came down on top of Grill. Jack fell on Shark. Both teens lost their balance and collapsed in the boat. Tech quickly pulled out his Paralaser. He aimed it directly at Max.

But this time, Max was ready for him. He swiftly kicked the device out of Tech's hand. It flew in the air and landed in the canal.

"That cost me a fortune!" raged Tech.

Tech let go of the propeller and lunged for Max. But Max was quicker. He rammed into Tech and shoved him off the back of the boat.

SPLASH!

The teen's head bobbed up above the waterline. He tried to catch up, but the boat was too fast.

"Arrrgh!" yelled Tech.

With Tech in the water, there was no one steering the boat. The boat chugged itself down the canal.

Out of nowhere, Grill pummeled into Max and thrust him on top of a fruit basket. He smashed Max's face into a bunch of mangoes.

At the same time, Jack was trying to wrench the cash off of Shark's back. He kicked Jack in the knee and threw him toward the edge of the boat. Jack's face was hanging over the edge, only inches from the water.

"You're going to pay for this!" scowled Shark as he tried to dunk Jack's face into the dirty canal.

Out of the corner of his eye, Jack spied another boat coming their way. On it was a man with a pet python. Once the man saw Jack's predicament, he steered his boat alongside Jack's. The man put his boat into neutral. Then, he lifted the

snake off of his shoulders and put it
onto Shark's.

"Aaaaahhhh!" squawked Shark, letting
go of Jack and flapping his hands like a
bird. "Get this thing off of me!"

The man laughed. So did Jack.

Jack grabbed a ball of twine from the
front of the boat and used it to tie
Shark's ankles and wrists together.

"*Kawp khun kap*," said Jack to the man.

The man smiled, removed the python
from Shark, and carried on down the
canal. The teen
exhaled and
collapsed in relief.

"Why you—"
growled Grill as he
let go of Max and
went after Jack.

Grill shoved Jack
onto his back. "I'm

going to take care of you once and for all," spat Grill, as he reached down for him.

But before Grill could do anything, something round and brown landed on his head. It splintered over him, so that Grill's dazed face popped out from underneath.

Max continued to shove its frame down over Grill's body until it wedged itself just above his elbows. Now, Grill couldn't use his arms to attack. When Jack saw what it was, he laughed. Max had apprehended Grill with one of the old lady's fruit baskets.

Chapter 20
The Swarm

After tying Grill's hands together with the remaining twine, Max took the propeller and guided the boat (and the criminals) back to the dock. An army of police were waiting for them. They swarmed the boat and arrested Grill and Shark. Then, they fished Tech out of the water.

When the police opened the two backpacks, they found the *Emerald Buddha* and the $300,000. They couldn't believe that a couple of kids had nabbed the crooks.

As Jack and Max climbed out of the boat, an older Thai policeman greeted them. Jack and Max put their hands together and bowed to the man. It was customary in Thailand to do this for people who were older than you.

"I'm Chief of Police Jaidee," said the man, extending his hand. "The GPF told us the crooks would be here at the market. Excellent work."

"Thanks," said Max.

Over the next ten minutes, Jack and Max told Chief Jaidee what had happened. They also told him about Larry. The chief downloaded an image of the man from Jack's phone. He then instructed his officers to hunt the man down.

"I think it's time we get you back to your parents," said Chief Jaidee. "I'm sure they're getting worried about you."

As they made their way to the chief's car, Jack and Max noticed the teenage gang. They were being dragged by the wrists into one of the vans. Grill gritted his silver teeth at the Stalwarts. Shark and Tech were looking miserable.

"Hope you enjoy your time in prison," said Jack as he smiled.

"Just remember," added Max, "bad guys *always* finish last."

Chapter 21
The Reunion

Chief Jaidee escorted Jack and Max to the
Grand Palace. He spoke to the officer at
the entrance, who stepped aside to let
Jack and Max through. The chief turned
to say his good-byes.

"Thanks again for everything," he said.

"Our pleasure," said Max.

"If there's anything we can do for
you," said the chief, "please let us
know."

The brothers thought for a moment.

"Could you keep our names and photos out of the news?" asked Jack.

Jack and Max didn't want their parents to know about their involvement. They also didn't want the mastermind to know what they looked like.

"Sure thing," said the chief. "I'll take care of it."

Jack and Max entered the palace grounds and made their way to the Temple of the Emerald Buddha. The police had just opened the exits. As soon as the boys stepped through the doorway, Corinne and John stood up.

Their mother rushed over. She hugged them tightly. Jack and Max thought they were going to burst.

"I was so worried about you," she gushed. "I'm glad you're okay."

Max's clothes were still a bit damp

from his dip in the river. Before his mum could ask about it, he came up with an excuse.

"We've been sweating out there for hours!" he said, thumbing to the previously blocked exits.

"You poor things!" said Corinne, fixing the boy's messed-up hair.

An instruction rang out on the police

officer's radios. As soon as they heard it, they left the floor of the temple.

"They must have recovered the Buddha," said John.

"I wonder who found it," said Corinne.

Jack and Max winked at each other.

"Never mind," said Corinne, waving her hand. "I'm sure we'll hear all about it on the news. What do you say we head to that market and do some shopping?"

"What do you say we do some *eating*," said John. "I'm starving!"

Jack and Max laughed. Their dad was always cracking jokes.

Chapter 22
The Future

Over the next hour, the Stalwarts
sampled all sorts of sweet and savory
snacks from the market. They tried
durian, the "smelliest fruit in the world,"
and another sweeter fruit called a
mangosteen. The clan even munched on
a couple of fried crickets.

As soon as they were alone, Max
turned to Jack.

"Were you serious about returning to the GPF?" asked Max.

Jack nodded. "I kind of miss it," said Jack. "Plus, we're good at what we do. The world needs us."

Max thought about what Jack had said. He agreed. "Let's tell Director Barter that we're going to be agents again when we get home."

"What are you going to do when you get home?" asked Corinne, walking up to the boys. She'd overheard the tail end of their conversation.

"We—uh," said Jack, not knowing quite what to say.

"We're going to post our favorite photos from the trip online!" said Max, thinking quickly.

"Great idea," said Corinne. "Let's start with this one."

Corinne told her family to huddle up. She held her camera high in the air, so that the Thai market was in the background.

"Everybody say 'fried crickets'!" she said.

"Fried crickets!" they said.

Then, Corinne snapped another photo of their adventure in Thailand.

Chapter 23
The Master Threat

Something was wrong. The mastermind's "collector" was supposed to text him two hours ago to say that he had the *Emerald Buddha*.

There was a knock at the door. It was his secretary, Linda. She was holding a piece of paper. "I think you should see this, sir," she said.

She handed the paper to the man. Almost as soon as she did, she hurried out of the room. The man's icy-blue eyes scanned the news report.

BREAKING NEWS

An attempt to steal Thailand's Emerald Buddha was thwarted today, thanks to the heroic actions of two boys. The boys managed to track the thieves and rescue the statue, which is now in the hands of the Thai authorities.

Three male teenagers have been arrested for the theft and are currently being interrogated by the police. An adult male, also linked to the crime, was identified from video footage and later arrested at the Hua Lamphong train station trying to escape.

"We can't thank these children enough," said Sunti Jaidee, Chief of the Royal Thai Police. "Without their help, we may never have seen the Emerald Buddha again."

The boys' names and pictures have been withheld in order to protect their privacy.

The man tried to stay calm, but a wave of rage came over him. He crumpled the paper into a ball and slammed his fist onto his desk.

The force of the strike caused a glass thermometer to fall on the floor and shatter into pieces. He looked down at the broken keepsake. It was a gift from his mother. He roared in anger.

"That's another thing you've cost me!" he shouted to the boys he'd never met. "Thanks to you, I've lost millions. What am I going to tell my client? Whoever you are," he seethed, "you're going to pay."

There was a knock again. It was Linda. "Everything all right, sir?" she asked. Her voice was gentle and calm.

"I'm fine," he grumbled.

He heard Linda's footsteps walk away from the door.

The man couldn't believe this turn of events. He'd hired a gang of highly skilled crooks and a collector that he trusted. How could this have happened?

The man opened the right drawer of his desk, and plucked another prepaid phone from inside. He dialed the phone number of his mole, or spy, at the GPF. In his line of business, it was wise to have people working "on the inside." The mole answered.

"Hello," said the agent nervously. The agent was expecting the call.

"What happened in Thailand?" growled the man.

"I don't know," said the mole. "The kids didn't come from us. Our agent was recalled."

The mastermind murmured something under his breath. Then, he hung up. At least that was a bit of good news.

In the meantime, he had to find another object for his Chinese client. Perhaps one of the items sitting in his office would appeal. If not, there were others to choose from.

He lifted a piece of paper from his desk and reviewed his "master list."

Three of the items were already his. They were the ones sitting in his office. But there were still more objects left to take.

A wicked smile spread across the mastermind's face. He thought about his goody-two-shoes brother, Gerald. Gerald had spent his life protecting the very treasures the man was after. If only his brother knew what the man was up to and which treasures were next on his list. At that thought, the mastermind leaned back in his pricey leather chair and laughed.

**Read more about
Jack and Max's adventures!**